THE
Nº1 CAR
SPOTTER
and the Car Thieves

by Atinuke

illustrated by Warwick Johnson Cadwell

WALKER
BOOKS

First published in Great Britain 2012 by Walker Books Ltd
87 Vauxhall Walk, London SE11 5HJ

2 4 6 8 10 9 7 5 3 1

Text © 2012 by Atinuke
Illustrations © 2012 Warwick Johnson Cadwell

The right of Atinuke and Warwick Johnson Cadwell to be identified as
author and illustrator respectively of this work has been asserted by them
in accordance with the Copyright, Designs and Patents Act 1988

This book has been typeset in Stempel Schneidler and WJCadwell

Printed and bound in Great Britain by Clays Ltd, St Ives plc

British Library Cataloguing in Publication Data:
a catalogue record for this book is
available from the British Library

ISBN 978-1-4063-2080-0

www.walker.co.uk

For Mama Akara –
and all of the ancestors
who live on in me and my boys
A.

To my gang as ever,
D, S, H and W
W. JC.

The No. 1 Car Spotter
in the Palm Tree

Heh – look up in the palm tree!

Is me! Oluwalase Babatunde Benson, otherwise known as No. 1, *the* No. 1!

You remember this bush village where I live? You remember my friends Coca-Cola and Emergency and Tuesday? You remember Grandmother and Grandfather? And Mama? And my sister Sissy? I can point them all out to you from up here in the tree. Look!

See Coca-Cola, pushing his wheelbarrow of soft drinks up from the river to his mother, Mama Coca-Cola. She is busy frying akara at her No. 1 chop-house road-side restaurant.

Emergency and Tuesday are throwing nets into the river with their father, Uncle Go-Easy! Their sister, Nike, and my sister, Sissy, are carrying firewood back to our cooking fires!

Grandfather is observing everybody
and everything from the shade of
the iroko tree. And Grandmother,
Mama and the aunties are busy
with the new palm oil press!

From high up in
this palm nut tree I can see
the village, I can see the
river, I can see the bush.
And most important of all,
I can see the road! And all
the fine-fine cars that pass.

"Mercedes-Benz ML 320! Peugeot 505!
VW Jetta!"

I know them by their engines before
I even see them. That is why I am called
No. 1. I am the No. 1 car spotter in my
village. I spot all cars. I shout their
names. When Mama Coca-Cola
hears me shout, she turns up
the cooking fires.

By the time the vehicles near the chop-house, the smell of frying chicken and akara and goat meat has fully penetrated the air conditioning systems of the vehicles.

The cars brake. They stop right outside the No. 1 chop-house. The drivers cannot help themselves. Their stomachs are now ruling the brake pedal. The people in the Mercedes and the Jetta jump out and go into the chop-house.

It is thanks to me that Mama Coca-Cola has a chop-house. Thanks to me Mama Coca-Cola now has customers who drive Mercedes-Benz. This means she can charge more than ten times the amount for her

akara than she could before, when her customers had to squat by the side of the road. And now that Mama Coca-Cola is making good money, come January, my tight friend Coca-Cola will be able to go to school! He will learn ABC. He will learn 1-2-3 – just like you – and when he grows up he will be a big man!

I am so happy for my best friend Coca-Cola. I am so proud of him. When he is a big man, we will live together in the city in his fine house and we will continue our car spotting. But instead of spotting cars in the road, we will be spotting cars parked in his own garage! BMW! Land Cruiser! Porsche!

"No. 1!" Grandmother shouts. "Are you picking palm nuts or are you catching flies?"

"He is spotting cars!" Sissy shouts back angrily under her load of firewood.

My sister Sissy thinks car spotting should be banned by the government.

She is angry that I am up in the cool breeze while she is sweating on the hot ground doing all the jobs that we normally share. Collecting firewood and water, grazing the goats in the bush, watering the cows at the river, sweeping the compound.

Sissy would rather be high in the cool trees picking palm nuts than down on the hot ground carrying heavy loads. But Grandmother says Sissy is a big girl now, too big to climb trees.

"No. 1!" Grandmother shouts again. "If you do not start picking palm nuts, you will be sleeping in that tree tonight. Because none of us are moving from here until my palm oil jars are full!"

I start to pick nuts quick-quick.

"Lamborghini DIABOLO!" I hear Coca-Cola screech.

My eyes turn immediately to the road.

A bright red Lamborghini is flying towards the village!

Mama Coca-Cola turns up the fire and the speed machine slows. It parks in front of the chop-house. A woman in a white dress emerges.

13

With customers like this, Mama Coca-Cola will be able to charge twenty times the amount for her akara. She will be able to send Coca-Cola to school in the US of A!

Two men in blue suits leave the chop-house. I saw them when they jumped out of their Jetta. Now one jumps into the Jetta and the other jumps into the Lamborghini. They both drive off.

My mouth falls open.

"No. 1!" Grandmother shouts once more. "What is wrong with you?"

My lips move but no sound comes out.

The woman in white comes out of the chop-house. She looks at the place where she had parked her Lamborghini. She looks around. She starts to scream.

Emergency and Tuesday and Uncle
Go-Easy have dropped their fishing nets.
Grandfather is struggling to his feet. I slide
down from the palm tree.

"No. 1!" Grandmother is still
shouting. "I am warning you!"

"Quiet," says Grandfather as
he hobbles over. "Something has
happened here, something more
important than palm oil."
Grandmother is speechless.

The police arrive. They question me. They question all of us. We all saw it happen. But we cannot help the police. None of us has ever seen the men in blue suits or the Jetta before.

Eventually the Lamborghini
woman departs in a battered
yellow taxi with its
doors held on by rope.

"I will never eat
here again! Never!"
she shouts at Mama Coca-Cola.

The next morning, before the sun has
even passed the horizon, I am back in the
palm tree.

"Today I want to see palm nuts,"
Grandmother orders. "No matter if cars are
stolen left, right and centre!"

Uncle Go-Easy, Emergency and Tuesday
are picking palm nuts today. Fish needs
palm oil to fry. Coca-Cola is in the trees as
well. Akara needs palm oil too.

Only Sissy and Nike are sweating on the
hot ground. Sissy narrows her eyes and
sucks her teeth.

It is so early in the morning even the road is slow. Only mammy-wagons rumble up and down. The one they call *Always Willing* stops first. Its passengers climb down to eat akara, squatting by the roadside.

Then cars start to pass.

"Peugeot 504," I whisper so Grandmother does not hear me. "Santana."

The cars park in front of the chop-house. People get out to buy akara. The men from the Peugeot eat in their car. I can see them busy on one tiny-tiny laptop.

"Honda Accord. Golf. Daewoo."

"Rolls-Royce Phantom!"

Our mouths are open, our hands are frozen.

A uniformed driver gets out and opens the back door of the Rolls. A big man in a chief's agbada robes enters the chop-house to sit on a chair and buy his akara at prices as inflated as his agbada. His driver goes around the back to buy his own akara at a more affordable price.

"Dat car shine pass Saturday night shoes!" Tuesday whispers. Grandmother looks up. We start to pick nuts again quick-quick. But I keep one eye on the chop-house. I have seen that chief before. In the newspaper!

In the Peugeot the two men are still busy on their laptop. Then one of them jumps out. He jumps into the Rolls. The Peugeot and the Rolls Royce drive off at top speed.

The akara falls out of the chief's driver's mouth.

"TIEF!" I shout. "TIEF! TIEF!"

People pour out of the chop-house. But by the time the chief emerges, his Rolls Royce is gone. There is only his driver running up the empty road with his mouth still open.

I slide down the palm tree and jump to the ground. Coca-Cola, Emergency, Tuesday and Uncle Go-Easy all follow me. *Thump! Thump! Thump! Thump!* Like ripe fruits falling to the ground.

"Not again!" wails Grandmother.

When I tell the police what I saw, the chief shakes his fist at me. "Useless boy!" he shouts. "Why did you not stop them? Why did you not shout quicker?"

* * *

That night my brain is alive with electricity.
I whisper to Sissy. She shakes her head.

"You must be crazy," she whispers back.

But the current is flowing, and I have
no OFF switch. I keep whispering and
whispering until Sissy agrees.

The next day I am in the palm
nut tree before cock-crow.

Sissy is wandering along the
side of the road with the hungry
goats. If Grandmother sees her she
will send her into the bush, where
the sweetest grasses grow.

But Grandmother is fighting with the
palm oil press. It is refusing to work.

"Foolish machine!" Grandmother growls.

"What will we do?" cries Auntie Fine-
Fine.

"We have not even finished paying for it!"
My mother has her head in her hands.

Then I see something.

"Firebird!" I shout.

"Firebird! Firebird!"

There is only one Pontiac Firebird in this our country. It is owned by a university professor. A man who stops in our village to eat akara and show us the newspapers. Once he even gave me a ride in his car!

"Firebird!" I shout again, ignoring Grandmother's narrowed eyes.

Following the Firebird is a Volkswagen Golf. Soon a Mercedes V-Boot and a Hummer HT3 join them in front of the chop-house.

Almost everybody gets out of their cars.
Prof waves to me and I wave back. The men
in the V-Boot are still in their car. They
open a laptop.

Grandmother, Mama and the aunties are
silent. They are looking at the broken palm
oil press. The money we have spent on it is
wasted and we haven't finished paying yet!

Suddenly I hear the
Hummer's doors opening.
A man jumps out of the
V-Boot and into the
Hummer.

The thieves gun
their engines and
speed away!

"TIEF! TIEF! TIEF!"

I shout as loud as I can.

Sissy hears me!

She drives the goats into the road right
in front of the speeding cars. Grandmother
screams.

"Don't worry!" I shout. "Sissy knows
what she is doing!"

But the speeding cars do not slow down.

They drive straight into the goats.

Dust flies up everywhere.

I jump straight down from the tree
SMACK! onto the hard ground. For one
second I cannot breathe. Then I look up
and see Sissy. She is lying by the side
of the road. Grandmother and Mama
are screaming.

"Sissy! Sissy! SISSY!"

I reach her first.
I wrap my arms
around my sister.

"Did we
catch'am?"
she whispers.

Grandmother
and Mama are
leaning over us.

"Who told you!"
Grandmother screams
at Sissy. "Who told
you to do such a
stupid thing?"

I hide behind Mama. Everybody has come running from the village to see if Sissy is OK.

"This boy!"

Grandmother is shouting for everybody to hear. She looks angrier than I have ever seen in my life.

"This boy asked my granddaughter to go and kill herself. For what? For a car! A *car*!"

"*Na-wa-oh*, mama!" says a bus driver.

Everybody looks at me. I hang my head and start to cry.

"We thought the thieves would stop if the goats blocked the road." Sissy is crying too.

"Unbelievable." The Hummer driver shakes his head. "These children are very brave."

"They just do not understand how bad people can be," says the professor sadly.

Now Grandmother starts to cry as well!

The Hummer driver takes his wallet out of his pocket.

"Your grandchildren tried to save my car," he says to Grandmother. "Let me reward them."

Grandmother opens her mouth to refuse. But Mama points to the broken palm oil press. So Grandmother takes the money and puts it in her blouse for safe-keeping.

"God will bless you," she says to the driver.

He has lost his car and still he rewarded us.

Then Grandmother grabs my ear and leads me back to our compound.

Mama rubs Sissy with medicinal oil.
Sissy was not hit by the cars. She was
knocked over by the goats as they ran.
One goat was killed.

"From now on," Mama says to Sissy, "you
are back up in palm trees where I can keep
my eye on you." Sissy smiles.

That night everybody eats goat meat apart
from me. I am in the house alone, sitting on
my mat.

Maybe that chief was right.

Maybe I am just
a useless boy.
A useless
village boy.

Then Sissy comes in with a bowl of
food. "No. 1," she whispers. "Tomorrow
Grandmother will remember that it was you
who got the money to fix the palm oil press.
You are truly the No. 1!"

"And tomorrow," Sissy continues "I will
be the one in the cool trees and you will be
collecting firewood."

Sissy smiles a big smile. It's so good to see
my sister alive and smiling, I can't help
it, I smile too. I smile my
No. 1 smile!

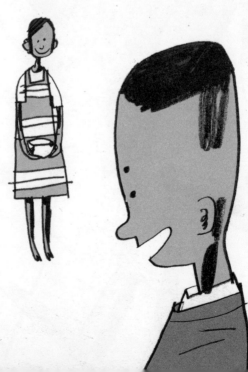

No. 1 Opens His Big Mouth

I am No. 1 at spotting cars. Almost every day I spot another one stolen.

First I spot the thieves busy on their laptops. Then I spot them steal a car. How are they overriding the cars' security systems?

"A-beg, use that No. 1 brain," says Coca-Cola.

"Make we catch dese thieves!" says Tuesday.

"With one No. 1 plan!" says Emergency.

But the thought of Sissy lying in the dust has jammed my brain's operating system.

Anyway, what can a boy in a palm tree do against a man with a laptop?

Prof reads to us from the newspapers. It is not just here where cars are being stolen.

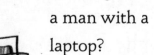

"Cars are being stolen from all over the country," Prof says. "Cities and towns and villages, the same. It is a national problem. The chief of police himself is on the case."

Prof looks at me. "Don't let your friends vex you, No. 1. This is a rich man's problem. Do you people have a car for thieves to steal?"

All of us laugh. The only car in our village broke down here and the owner never came to take it away. Thanks to one of my No. 1 ideas it is now the village cart.

But when Prof is gone the other boys keep on vexing me. Even Uncle Go-Easy, even Grandfather wants me to tackle those thieves.

"I don't know where you are hiding that No. 1 brain of yours!" says Uncle Go-Easy.

"You have more brains than all those thieves put together!" says Grandfather.

"O-ya," says Mama Coca-Cola. "You don't have to solve the whole national whatever, just stop the thieves from operating here."

"It is not my problem," I say.

Grandfather raises his eyebrows.

"It is a rich man's problem," I say.

"You think a problem can be one person's alone?" Grandfather asks me.

He shakes his head.

"What affects one of us affects us all. We are one human race!"

"I am only saying what Prof says," I say.

But maybe Grandfather is right. Every time a fine-fine car is stolen from outside the chop-house and the owner is forced to leave in a battered old taxi, it is Mama Coca-Cola that they blame.

"I will not eat here again!" they shout. "Useless ye-ye woman! Don't you know about security? Don't you have surveillance camera?"

Us, who do not even have electricity! It pains Mama Coca-Cola. It pains all of us.

Prof reassures her. "Cars are being stolen from outside all restaurants and schools, even hospitals!"

"So why do they blame me!" Mama Coca-Cola wails.

"It will soon stop, it will soon stop," Prof says calmly. "The chief of police himself is on the case."

Mama Coca-Cola sucks her teeth. "I do not see the chief of police here."

"But he is widening the net, he is widening the net." Prof is reading from the newspaper.

"Is the chief of police a fisherman?" I joke. "If so, I hope he knows how to throw his net well-well. A speeding Mercedes is hard to catch."

Everybody laughs loud. Uncle Go-Easy stands up and pretends to throw an imaginary net.

"I go catch one million dollar fish!" he shouts.

Even Prof is laughing.

* * *

The next day I am down at the river,
watering the cows. Uncle Go-Easy is
catching fish with Emergency
and Tuesday.

"TIEF! TIEF!" I hear
Coca-Cola shout.
I turn towards the chop-house.
A Range Rover Overfinch is
speeding away. A fat man in a
fine agbada is trying to run
up the road.

The Range Rover is almost level with
me now. I can see a man hunched
over the wheel.

"TIEF!"

Uncle Go-Easy
throws his net.
It flies through
the air and lands on
the speeding Range Rover.
The car swerves off the
road and into the bush.
Uncle Go-Easy is pulled off his
feet. The car speeds through the
bush. Uncle Go-Easy is dragged behind it.
His arm tangled in the net.

I see Emergency and Tuesday run
screaming towards their father.
People are running from
the chop-house and
the village.

I stand where I am. I see the net tear on a tree. I see the Range Rover drive back onto the road and away, fast. I see them carry Uncle Go-Easy to the village. I see blood.

Slowly I take the cows back to the compound. Grandfather is there.

"It is not your fault, No. 1!" he says.

I say nothing. I go into the dark house. I sit on my mat.

After a while I hear Mama and Sissy and Grandmother come in crying.

"They have taken him to the hospital," Mama says.

Then I hear Grandmother say, "Why does that boy have to put his stupid ideas into everybody's heads!"

I lie down on my mat. When my mother comes to call me for food, I do not answer her.

From now on I sit under the iroko
tree with Grandfather. I do not talk.
I do not laugh. I do not spot cars.

There are no good cars to spot anyway.
The rich people have decided to stay at
home. Whenever they go out, people
steal their cars.

Mama Coca-Cola's chop-house
is quiet now. She has plenty-plenty
customers still. But only the ones who

prefer to squat outside
in the shade. Only
the ones who can
pay small-small for
their food. The ten-
times, twenty-times
customers are at
home, eating
their own akara.

"No. 1," Grandfather says, "you cannot blame yourself for other people's actions."

But if I had not opened my mouth, Uncle Go-Easy would never have tried to catch a speeding car with his fishing net.

And he would not be in hospital now. And his daughter Nike would not be there looking after him.

And his sons Emergency and Tuesday would not be catching fish day and night to pay for medicine.

And Mama and Sissy would not be herding their goats and cows. Soon those goats and cows will have to be sold to pay for hospital bills. When Uncle Go-Easy comes out he will have nothing. And no matter what Grandfather says, I know it is the fault of my big mouth.

"Firebird!" It is Coca-Cola
shouting.

He is bringing soft drinks from
the river in his wheelbarrow for
Mama Coca-Cola's customers. I know,
and he knows, and Mama Coca-Cola
knows, that unless the rich customers
return, Coca-Cola will never go to school.
He will not become a rich man and live in
a fine house and drive his own car. He will
push a wheelbarrow of soft drinks for the
rest of his life.

Prof parks his car. He looks at the empty
chop-house. He turns to where I am sitting
with Grandfather under the iroko tree.

"I had thought this was only a
rich man's problem," says Prof,
"but I can see I was wrong."
Grandfather nods
his head.

"One person's problem is always everybody's problem," he says.

"But what about the poor?" Prof asks. "When the poor suffer, they suffer alone."

Grandfather looks at Prof.

"You are an educated man," he says. "Your parents had the money to send you to school. And now you are in a position to help our whole country. But what if your parents had been poor. Would you even be able to help yourself?"

"But if I had been poor, who would have suffered apart from me?" Prof says.

"The whole country would have suffered!" Grandfather says loudly. "From the loss of a great teacher. Everybody you have ever taught or inspired would have lost.

"Everybody suffers from poverty. From the loss of teachers and doctors who could have saved lives, leaders and inventors who could have made lives better. Instead, those clever ones are struggling in poverty just to feed themselves. Maybe they have even become armed robbers and thieves!

"Believe me," says Grandfather. "The whole world suffers from poverty."

Prof is silent for a long time. He looks at the sky and the one cloud that is slowly passing and the goats that are chewing.

At last he says, "Baba, you are right. Why did my universities not teach me this? I have been to Harvard, to Oxford, to UniLag. Nobody spoke of this."

Grandfather laughs. "There is a difference between what is taught in the university and what an old man knows. One is education, the other is wisdom."

Grandfather laughs again. "I myself do not know how to read or write. Not even my name." He opens his arms wide. "Life is what will bring you wisdom," he says, "if you pay attention."

Prof is silent, nodding. Then he looks at me.

"Come on, No. 1," he says. "Try to smile. You have not been alone in failing. Even the chief of police himself cannot stop those car thieves!"

I say nothing. I am not sad about failing. I am sad for Uncle Go-Easy and Emergency and Tuesday and Nike.

"No. 1 has not stopped trying," says Grandfather. "He has not stopped trying to stop those thieves."

I look at Grandfather. He is wrong!

"You had better be wrong," says Grandmother, passing the tree. "Because if that boy tries again, the chief of police himself will not be able to save him from me!"

Prof looks at my face and laughs.

"Come on, No. 1!" he says. "Let us go for a ride in my car!"

"Na-wa-oh!" I jump to my feet. My engine is running, my pistons are going. Prof has overriden my security systems and turned on my ignition.

I run down to the Firebird. The seats are smooth and shiny and clean. Much cleaner than my torn and dirty shorts.

"Don't worry, No. 1!" Prof laughs.

So I jump in.

Now that my engine is going, maybe
my brain will think of something to help
Uncle Go-Easy and his children.

Something No. 1!
To save my friends!

The No. 1 Car Spotter
Is Stolen

I am the No. 1 car spotter in the No. 1 car, driving down the No. 1 road.

There is only one No. 1 car spotter in my whole village. Only one Pontiac Firebird in my whole country. And there is only one road like this in the whole world.

This road goes to the capital city in
this my country. It goes through many big-
big towns. It passes uncountable villages.

Last time I rode in the Firebird, we went
to the nearest town. This time Prof drives in
the other direction.

"How about it, No. 1?" he says. "Do you
want to see the city?"

I leap up so high in my seat that my head
hits the roof. I have never seen the city!

Prof laughs.

I have heard many-many stories about it.
In the city people wear fine-fine clothes

every day. Every shop and chop-house
has lights that flash and dazzle all night.
Cars drive up and down, up and down,
pumping out loud music.

And now I am here. In the city! For the
very first time! I twist about in my seat with
my eyes popping from my head. Everything
I have heard, it is all true!

"Let us stop here to buy pizza," Prof says,
"before your neck twists off your body."

Prof parks outside a chop-house with a
red flashing sign. PIZZA HUT.

He looks at my torn and dirty shorts. Prof sighs and I know why.

In the village my clothes are exactly what is required for collecting firewood and herding goats. My fine-fine clothes are stored in the bottom box in my mother's room. They are only for weddings and parties. But here in the city, my clothes make me look like a beggar boy. I cannot enter Pizza Hut like this.

"Wait here, No. 1," Prof says. "I will go and get us pizza. We can eat in the car."

"OK, sa'!" I say.

Nothing can make me sad today. I am in the city!

"And watch my car for me," Prof says. "Don't let those car thieves take it."

"OK, sa'!" I laugh. "Yes, sa'!"

When Prof has gone into Pizza Hut I jump into the back of the car. There is a new Esclade parked behind us I want to see.

When I jump on the back seat I knock Prof's briefcase onto the floor. It opens and papers spill under the seats. What will Prof say? I squeeze onto the floor to reach the papers. Then the driver's door opens. Prof is back already!

Then the passenger door opens as well. Before I can move, a voice speaks.

"Drive'am, drive'am!"

"Hurry, hurry!" says the voice from the passenger seat again.

"Don' hassle me, man," says the driver. "You think I no sabi drive?"

But that is not Prof's voice. Neither of them is Prof's voice. There are two men in the car and neither of them is Prof. I am on the floor, my body stiff like firewood. The Firebird zooms off.

I open my mouth to shout. "Be quiet, No. 1," orders my brain. "You saw what these people did to Sissy and Uncle Go-Easy." My mouth closes.

"Tonight," says the first man, "we escape with all the cars. The ship is ready. This is the last car we steal. Nobody can catch us now!" He laughs.

Then I remember Grandfather saying, "No. 1 has not finished trying. He has not finished trying to catch those car thieves."

But it is not true. I have not caught the car thieves. It is they who have caught me.

"Do you not think the police are watching the harbour?" the driver asks.

"Many ships will be loading cars tonight," answers the first voice. "Nobody will know ours are stolen. Anyway," he says with a laugh, "we will take the chief of police a message. To make him look the other way."

"Wha' kin' of message?" the driver asks.

"That the stolen cars are leaving the country tonight," the first man replies. "In convoy across the desert!"

The thieves laugh. The car drives for a long time. I am shaking with fear. Will they load me onto a ship too? Will I ever see Mama and Sissy and Grandfather again? Suddenly I hear creaking and groaning, like the sound of our old wooden village cart, but louder.

The car slows. We drive into a dark and quiet place. The Firebird stops.

"This is the last car," the driver says. "And it is a good one. When we sell all of these cars overseas we will be rich. Rich!"

"O-ya," says the passenger. "Let us eat before we take the chief his message."

The two men jump out. They slam the doors. I hear their footsteps walk away. My brain goes into gear.

"O-ya, le's go," it says. "Unless you want to be loaded onto that ship tonight!"

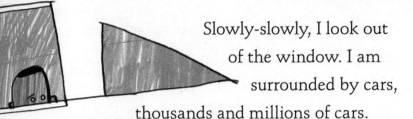

Slowly-slowly, I look out
of the window. I am
surrounded by cars,
thousands and millions of cars.
In a building with no windows. I can see
nobody. I can hear nobody. I want to get
back to my village – even if I have to run all
the way. I have had enough of city life!

My hand pulls the door handle. The door
opens silently. I crawl out of the Firebird.
My body is so stiff, so paining. I crawl
between the cars. Yellow Porche 911,
black BMW X-5, red Mercedes ML 320.

I pass behind an SUV with an open door. Suddenly I hear voices. The thieves' voices!

"HIDE NOW!" my brain screams.

I jump in and climb through to the back of the SUV. I roll into a ball. The thieves get in. I am trapped again, with the thieves.

"Leaving the door open makes it cooler," says one.

"Le's go! Le's go!" says the other.

We drive out into the city. The car thieves have stolen me again! How am I supposed to catch them if they keep catching me?

Today I have been inside more cars than I have ever been in my life. But each time I have been shaking on the floor. This is not a No. 1 situation. "But you are the No. 1," my brain speaks up. "You have spotted the car thieves but they have not spotted you!"

The SUV stops but the engine is still running. The passenger is speaking to somebody.

"We have information for the chief," he says. "Confidential."

"Enter, enter!" a voice shouts.

Slowly we drive on. And park.

"When we have delivered our message," growls the passenger, "we will return to wait with the cars until we load them on the ship tonight!"

"And tomorrow we will be rich!" The driver laughs.

They get out, slamming the doors behind them.

I can hear car engines, reversing, parking,
starting up and quenching. I can hear
voices. But none of them near the SUV.
Carefully I look out.

I am in a yard full of policemen and
police cars! This must be the city police
station. Why have the thieves brought
me here?

Then I remember what they said: "A
message for the chief of police! To make
him look the other way!"

The thieves have come here to trick
the chief of police! To tell him that the cars
will leave the country across the desert.
Then he will not look towards the ships!

I must warn him. I must find the chief
of police and warn him now! Then the
thieves will be caught. The Firebird will
not be lost. The chief will return me to my
mother. The rich will come back and eat
in Mama Coca-Cola's chop-house again.
And Coca-Cola will go to school!

I jump out of the
SUV into the police
yard. Three big police cars,
sirens blasting, come screeching in front
of me. There is no time to run. There is no
time to hide. The cars stop.

A police officer jumps out of the front of
the biggest car. He opens the back door.
A small man in uniform gets out. He looks
at me.

"Since when were beggar boys allowed in my police yard?" he asks.

The police officer pushes me towards the gate.

"Commot! Go!" he says. "Did you not hear the chief?"

The chief? The small man is the chief of police! I need to speak to him! I dodge the police officer's arms. But the chief is disappearing into the police station. He is gone.

The police officer drags me to the gates.

Outside those gates, along with all the fine-fine people, are all the beggars in the world. Outside those gates the buildings reach to the sky and people sleep underneath rotting cardboard. A city like this can devour a small boy like me.

"Psss!"

The police officer turns around. It is the driver of the police chief's car who is calling.

"Make the beggar boy come wash the chief's cars!" he shouts.

The police officer lets go of me. I run back to the cars. I have escaped the teeth of the city. And maybe now I will see the chief again.

"Wash these cars," the driver says, "and I will give you money for akara."

Happily I take the bucket and cloth. The driver crawls onto the back seat of one of the cars to sleep.

Slowly I begin to wash the cars. Soon the chief of police will come out of his office. And I will still be here. Those thieves will tell him one thing but I will tell him another.

He will catch the thieves and I will catch a bus back to my village!

The No. 1 Car Spotter Spots the Car Thieves

I am the No. 1 car spotter.
Pretending to be a No. 1 beggar boy
washing the chief of police's cars.

The driver sleeps in the back seat
while I wash and polish. Polish and
wash. After a while the door at the
top of the police station bangs open.
Policemen all around the yard salute.

71

The police chief's driver leaps out of the car
and jumps to attention as well.

Out of the police station steps the chief
of police. And the
car thieves are
with him!

They are smiling and shaking hands with
him! He is smiling too!

I am so afraid.

I jump inside the back of the car where
the driver was sleeping. I crouch on the
floor. I hear the thieves' SUV drive away.

The chief of police is speaking. "Police officers, get into your cars," he says. "Tonight we apprehend the car thieves."

"Where, sir?" a policeman asks.

"That is confidential information," says the chief. "You will follow my car."

"Urgent telephone call, sir!" I hear somebody shout.

Two police officers jump into the front of the escort car. I crouch down lower. They don't see me.

"I have never seen the chief vex like this," one of them says.

"It is those car thieves," says the other, and he sucks his teeth. "People are saying the chief of police cannot stop them. Not even if they took his own car."

"If I find those thieves," says the first, "I will bang their heads together."

"No need." The other laughs. "You are a police officer. You can simply handcuff them and throw them into jail."

Both policemen laugh.

"I can find them for you!" somebody shouts.

Before I realize that it was me that shouted, there are two policemen looking down at me.

My brain puts its head in its hands.

The policemen look at me. I look at them.

"It is that beggar boy," says one of them to the other. "What are you doing in my police car?" he says to me.

"I know where the thieves are hiding the stolen cars," I say.

The police officers laugh loudly.

"And since when did we fraternize with beggar boys in my car?" shouts a loud voice.

All of us jump. It is the chief of police, come back out of the police station.

The police
officers jump
out of the car and
salute. I copy them.

"What is going
on here!" shouts
the chief.

Speak now! says my brain. But my mouth
is opening and closing like a fish's.

"We found this boy hiding in the back of
the car," says one of the policemen.

The police chief looks at me. "As if I do
not have enough on my hands!" he shouts.
"Take him away."

The policemen take hold of me.

My mouth retrieves my voice from my
stomach.

"The car thieves are trying to trick you!" I
croak. "They are escaping by ship tonight!"

But the chief of police is walking away.
And he does not stop.

"They will take all those fine-fine cars out of our country!" I am shouting now. "Even our only Firebird!"

The chief of police stops. He stands still. He turns back around to face me.

"What did you say?" he asks.

"They took Prof's car," I say. "He asked me to watch it. But I was too afraid to stop them."

"Chief, don't waste your time," says one of the policemen.

"Wait!" says the chief. "I had a call from Prof just now. He said his Firebird had been stolen. With a village boy inside!"

"This boy is probably working with the thieves," says the police officer.

I look at him.

"I am the No. 1 car spotter," I say. "The No. 1 car spotter in my village. I am NOT a car thief."

The chief of police smiles.

"That is exactly what Prof said," he says. "So you made your way to the police station to report the theft. You are a brave boy."

I shake my head.

"I am not brave," I said. "I was carried to the station in the back of the car thieves' car."

"What?" shouts the chief.

I tell the chief of police how I hid in the back of the Firebird and then in the back of the SUV.

"Those men who came to give you information," I say, "they are the car thieves."

"They are private detectives," the chief of police explains to me. "Working for a lady who has had more than five cars stolen."

"They are not detectives!" I shout. "They are car thieves!" The chief sighs.

"No. 1," he says. "Either I believe two grown men or I believe one small boy. I cannot be in two places at once tonight. The police force is already stretched thin."

"Sir," says a police officer. "How can what he says be true? How could he have been on the floor of all those cars without being noticed?"

"I was on the floor of your car." I eye him. "I heard you say that you would bang the heads of the thieves together."

The chief laughs. Then he sighs.

"I cannot go to the harbour because a small boy tells me to."

He pats my head.

And walks away.

"They are not going through the desert!"
I shout. "They are trying to trick you!"

The chief stops again. His back is stiff.

"What did you say?" he asks.

"The thieves are trying to trick you."
I am crying now. "They want you to go to
the desert so you do not see them escape
by ship."

The police officers look at each other.

"How do you know they told me to go
to the desert?" The chief looks at me hard.
"This is confidential information."

"I was hiding on the floor of the SUV
listening." I sob. "I heard them say they
were going to tell you about a
convoy across the desert so
that you would be far from
the harbour."

The chief of police takes
out his phone.

"Prof," I hear him say. "I have your No. 1 boy here."

"No. 1? Thank God!" I hear Prof say. Then I hear him shout, "They have found him! The police have found him!"

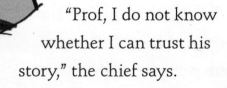

"Prof, I do not know whether I can trust his story," the chief says.

"You can trust him one hundred percent," says Prof. "He is a No. 1 boy."

The chief closes his phone and looks at me.

"He is a beggar boy," says one of the police officers. "Look at him."

"I am a village boy," I say. "I herd goats and carry firewood. I would be a foolish boy to do that in fine-fine clothes."

The chief smiles.

"Even if he was a beggar boy," he says to the police officer, "would that mean he did not have a brain?"

"A No. 1 brain!" I say.

"OK, No. 1." The chief of police laughs. "Tell me everything!"

So I tell the chief the whole story from the beginning. I even tell him how I think the thieves used their laptops to override the cars' security systems.

"Na-wa-oh!" the police officers gasp.

"You see," the chief of police tells them. "A No. 1 brain can take any disguise." Then he says, "Let us change our clothes. Night has come and we have thieves to catch."

It is true. As we have been talking, night has come. The stolen cars will be loading onto the ship any minute now!

The chief and police officers go inside. They leave me sitting outside. Somebody brings me akara and Coca-Cola! When the men come out I do not recognize them! Their uniforms are gone. They are wearing the clothes of labourers, old and torn. Their skin is dirty, their eyes are red.

"No. 1, we have copied your disguise." The smallest man winks.

We all follow him out of the side door of the compound. As we walk along the road the stink of the roadside gutter is strong in my nose. A mammy-wagon passes us. There are many men in the back with rough voices and dirty faces. When the wagon slows, the chief and his men jump into the back. I run and they pull me up too. Nobody looks at us.

I squat in the back of the bumping, bouncing lorry, holding on to the side. I keep my mouth shut.

When I hear creaking and groaning
I stand up. We are in a yard of big ships.
It is ships making this creaking and
groaning! Big lights show that cars are
being driven out of big-big buildings
and onto each ship.

But they cannot *all* be stolen cars!
Which ship is being loaded with
stolen cars?

The mammy-wagon slows.
Nobody looks at us. We are only
a broken lorry full of men who
have come to work and sweat.

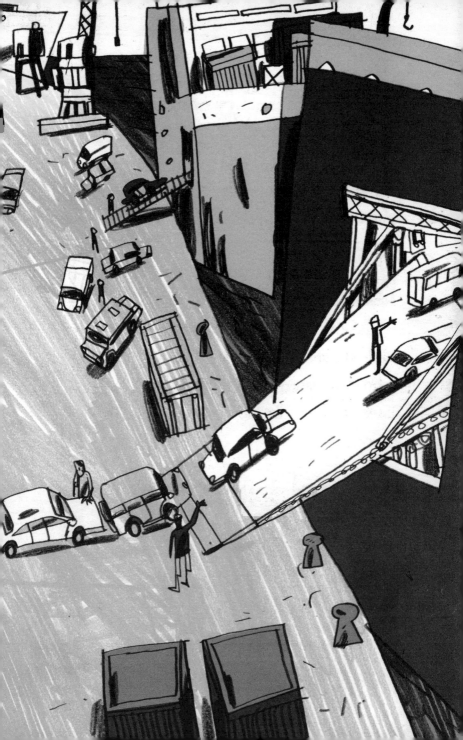

The chief squats on the floor next to me.
He looks into my eyes.

"We cannot make a mistake now," he
says. "You are the No. 1 car spotter. Spot
those stolen cars!"

I stand up. I do not look at the ships. I do not look at the buildings. I do not look at the men. I look at the cars.

Daewoos, Mercedes Benz, BMWs, Range Rovers, Lamborghinis, Nissans. There are so many-many cars. Then I spot a yellow Porsche 911, a black BMW X-5, a red Mercedes ML 320!

Those were the cars I saw in the building. The stolen cars!

The chief leans his ear to my mouth.

"Big orange ship," I whisper. "Longest line. I have seen those cars before."

The chief hesitates. "Are you sure?"

I am not sure! There may be many-many yellow Porsche 911s, black BMW X-5s, red Mercedes ML 320s in the shipyard.

Carefully I scan each line of cars entering the third ship. I spot each car. Then I see it!

The Firebird! The red Pontiac Firebird!

"There is only one Firebird in this country!" I point.

The chief and his men leap from the mammy-wagon. They scatter behind the buildings and run crouching along the lines of cars … and catch the car thieves!

"HANDS UP!" they shout.

* * *

Now it is morning. All night the police have
been busy rounding up car thieves.

"Let's have breakfast," says the chief.

"Pizza Hut?" I ask.

The chief laughs and slaps my back.
"Anything you say, No. 1."

We collect the pizza in the car of the
chief of police. And now I cannot wait to
see Mama and Sissy. I cannot wait to tell
Grandfather and Coca-Cola everything.

Maybe even Grandmother will have forgiven me by now.

She definitely will when she sees what I have in my pocket. An envelope with reward money. A reward big enough to pay for Uncle Go-Easy's hospital bills!

In the village everybody is waiting. Even Uncle Go-Easy!

Their eyes pop out of their heads when they see me arrive with the chief of police himself.

The chief shakes hands with Grandfather.

"I hear you trained this boy yourself," he says.

"It was a small thing," says Grandfather.

"A small thing?" says the chief. "From now on car spotting is of No. 1 national importance! And this is our No. 1 boy!"

Everybody cheers. They throw me in the air like I scored a World Cup goal.

I am the No. 1. The No. 1 car spotter. Not just in my own village, but in my whole entire country – maybe in the whole entire world.

I can spot a car fast enough to catch a thief!

Atinuke was born in Nigeria
and grew up in both Africa and the UK.
She collects traditional tales from Africa
and the African diaspora which she
performs in schools and theatres all over
the world. All of Atinuke's many children's
books are set in modern Africa. She lives
with her husband and sons on a mountain
overlooking the sea in Wales.

Warwick Johnson Cadwell lives
by the Sussex seaside with his smashing
family and pets. Most of his time is
spent drawing or thinking about drawing
but for a change of scenery he also
skippers boats. *The No. 1 Car Spotter
and the Car Thieves* is his fourth book
for Walker Books.